For Judy, My Wonderful Mother
- S.R.

With Love and Thanks to my Family
and "Happy Birthday" to my understanding Mom
- L.W.

I Love My Mommy
© 1995 by Scharlotte Rich
Illustrations © 1995 by Linda Weller

Requests for information should be addressed to:

Zonder**kidz** ™

The Children's Group of ZondervanPublishingHouse
Grand Rapids, Michigan 49530
www.zonderkidz.com

Zonderkidz is a trademark of The Zondervan Corporation
ISBN: 0-310-70103-1

I Love My Mommy was previously published by Gold-N-Honey, a division of Multnomah Publishers.

Printed in Singapore

00 01 02 03 04 05 /HK/ 10 9 8 7 6 5 4 3 2 1

Scharlotte Rich

I Love My Mommy!

ILLUSTRATIONS BY LINDA WELLER

Zonderkidz

The Children's Group of ZondervanPublishingHouse

Introduction

Mothers are like flowers.
They come in lots of different shapes,
sizes, and colors.

They live in many different
kinds of places.

They have many
different kinds of jobs.

$\mathcal{B}$ut one thing is always the same.
They have a very special place in their
hearts just for their children.

$\mathcal{I}$ have a very special mommy.
The first thing I hear in the morning
is my mommy saying,
"Good morning, Honey-bun."
That's what she calls me, because she says I'm
sweet enough to nibble on. Mommy says
I am her special gift from God.

We are alike in many ways.
She says my eyes are just like hers.
My hands look just like Mommy's, too.
We both like to eat pancakes
for breakfast. Mommy makes
funny faces on mine.

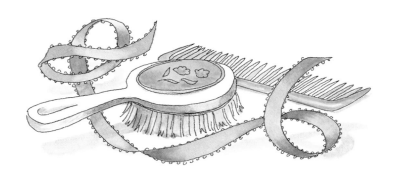

Some mornings, when it's warm,
we go out to work in the garden.
My garden is just like Mommy's garden.
She showed me how to plant seeds
and water them.

$\mathcal{I}$ waited for the seeds to grow.
They grew into big
sunflowers that are bigger than me!
Mommy says God put the flower inside
each little seed. I wonder how God does that!
Mommy says it's easy for Him because
God can do anything.

$\mathcal{I}$ asked Mommy if God made the
bugs and the little green snake in the garden.
She said, "Yes, and God made this fat
woolly caterpillar, too."

We get our hands
all dirty pulling up weeds.
Sometimes when I do something bad,
Mommy says, "That's like a little weed
growing in your garden.
You and God need to pull it up."

After Mommy and I fix lunch,
it's time for my nap. Mommy fixes me a special
place by the window where it's cool.
I pretend it's my castle.

I love my mommy, and my mommy loves me.
That's the way God planned it to be.

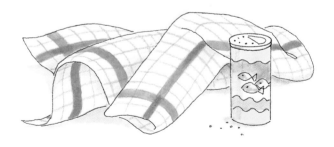

A Walk with Mommy

$\mathcal{I}$ woke up this morning
and something was different.
When I stuck my toes out of my nice warm bed,
the floor was as cold as ice.

My mommy said, "Well, Little Pumpkin,
summer is over. Let's take a long walk today
and see what fall looks like."

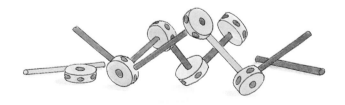

After breakfast, we put on our jackets and warm shoes and socks. I wanted to go barefoot, but Mommy said my feet would get too cold.

$\mathcal{W}$e packed peanut butter sandwiches and
big red apples in my backpack.
Then off we went.

$\mathcal{M}$ommy and I walked
past all the houses in our neighborhood.
We scuffled through the leaves
while we walked.

$\mathcal{T}$hen we came to the park.
Mommy pushed me on the swings,
and I went high up to the sky.

On top of the big slide I was a little afraid.
But Mommy said, "Don't worry, Little Sweet
Potato. I'll catch you."

So, down I went, faster and faster.
Mommy caught me, just in time!
She scooped me up in the air.

Then we walked down the path behind the park. The grass was taller than me, but not taller than my mommy.

Suddenly, Mommy stopped.
"*Shhh,*" she said. "Look over there!"
She pointed at two gray squirrels
with big fluffy tails.

"The squirrels are gathering
nuts so they will have food for the winter.
Then they'll dig holes and hide the
nuts in the ground

"How will they find them when it snows?" I asked. Mommy said God gave squirrels very special noses to find the nuts when their families are hungry.

"I'm hungry right now," I said.
So we sat down on
some big rocks and had a picnic,
just Mommy and me.

I love my mommy, and my mommy loves me.
That's the way God planned it to be.

A Rainy Day with Mommy

This morning I heard noise on our roof.
It sounded like lots of cats running
and jumping all over.

I ran to the window. It was raining outside.

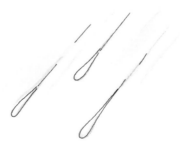

$\mathcal{I}$ got dressed and went downstairs.
My mommy was washing clothes.

"Good morning, Sunshine!" she said.
"It's so dark and gloomy outside.
Your smile will have to brighten up
our house today."

When I smiled she said,
"Wow!" and covered her eyes. "Your smile
is really bright! I'll need to get my sunglasses!"

My mommy likes to tease me.
I like to tease her, too.

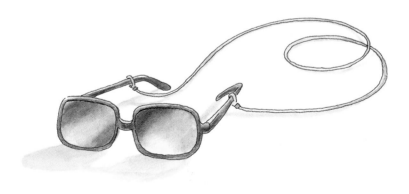

"Mommy," I said,
"what can I do today since it's raining outside?"

"I know," she said. "You can go camping."
"But Mommy, it's raining!"

"You can camp inside," said Mommy,
"but first we need a tent."

$\mathcal{M}$ommy helped me set up my tent.

Then I went upstairs and
brought down all of my favorite books.
I packed the books and some toys
in my suitcase.

$\mathcal{M}$ommy said,
"I think you need a fire to keep you warm."
So we built a fire with the flashlight
and some red tissue paper.
I told stories to the animals from
my picture books.

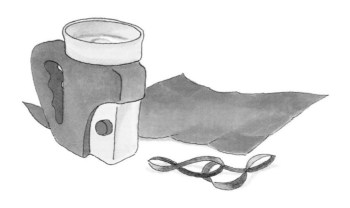

$\mathcal{T}$hen I cooked lunch
for the animals over the fire. They ate it all up
and growled and grumbled when I said
they couldn't have any more.
After lunch we played in the woods
for a long time.

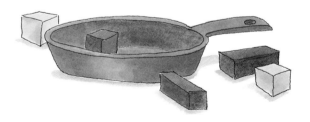

On the way home we splashed in the puddles.
We stuck out our tongues to taste the rain.
The rain made the air smell good.

"Why does God make rainy days?" I asked.

"God uses rain to give all the plants
and animals a drink when they're thirsty,"
Mommy said.
"That's how we get our water to drink, too."
I can't wait until I grow up
and know lots of things like Mommy.

I love my mommy, and my mommy loves me.
That's the way God planned it to be.

Bedtime with Mommy

We were playing outside
catching fireflies. I started to yawn.
Mommy said,
"It's time for bed, Sleepyhead."

So I began to get ready.
First I fed Fuzzy, our cat, and put water
in her bowl.

$\mathscr{N}$ext, I went upstairs to brush my teeth.
I have a toothbrush that sparkles.
Brush, brush, *kersplat!*

Then, I took a nice long bath.
Mommy put my duck and my boat
in the water with me.

Mommy washed my hair.
She made lots of funny shapes with
the shampoo.

$\mathcal{T}$hen she dried me off
with a big fluffy towel and I put on
my favorite jammies.

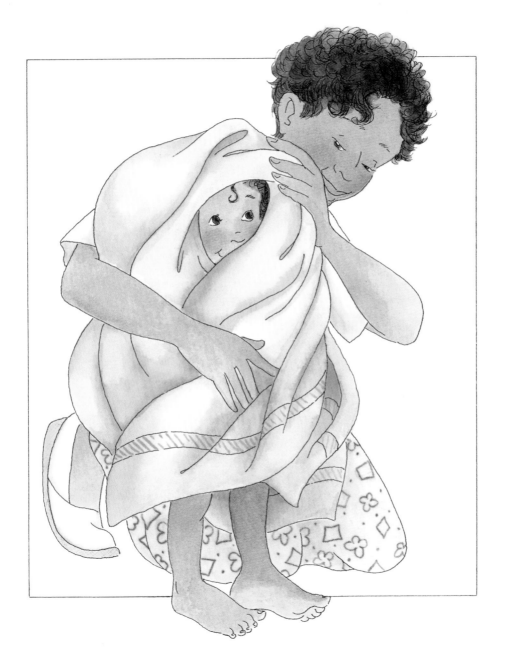

"Hop into bed, Little Chickadee,"
said Mommy.

"I need to say goodnight to all
the animals," I said.

$\mathcal{I}$ said goodnight to Bear and Elephant.
Then Mommy read me a Bible story.

$\mathcal{M}$ommy turned off the
lights and we prayed and talked together
in the dark for a while.
"Mommy, do you love me?" I said.
"Oh, yes," Mommy said softly.
"I love you *very* much."

"*B*ut Mommy,
do you love me even when I do *bad* things?"
I peeked out of one eye.
"Yes," she said, "Even when I'm angry with you,
I still love you."

"*M*ommy...*why* do you love me?"

"I love you for so many reasons I can't even
count them all. I love you just because you're
you. I love your nose, I love your eyes,
I love the you that you are inside."
She gave me a great big hug.

"Listen to this and always remember it:
The ocean isn't deep enough to hold all
the love I have for you."

"The sky isn't high enough
to hold all the love I have for you.
You will always have your own special place
right here in my heart. Now, close your eyes,
Little Mouse, and go to sleep."

I love my mommy, and my mommy loves me.
That's the way God planned it to be.